CHARLIE BUMPERS vs.

THE TEACHER OF THE YEAR

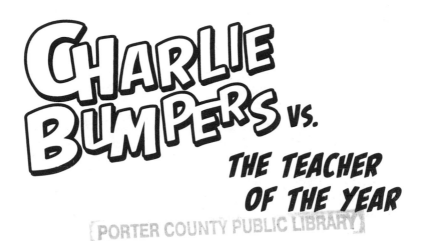

CHARLIE BUMPERS VS.

THE TEACHER OF THE YEAR

Bill Harley

Illustrated by Adam Gustavson

PEACHTREE

ATLANTA

Published by
PEACHTREE PUBLISHERS
1700 Chattahoochee Avenue
Atlanta, Georgia 30318-2112
www.peachtree-online.com

Design and composition by Nicola Simmonds Carmack

The illustrations were rendered in India ink and watercolor.

Printed in July 2013 by RR Donnelley & Sons in Harrisonburg, VA, in the United States of America
10 9 8 7 6 5 4 3 2 1
First Edition

Library of Congress Cataloging-in-Publication Data

Harley, Bill, 1954-
  Charlie Bumpers vs. the Teacher of the Year / by Bill Harley ; illustrated by Adam Gustavson.
    pages cm
  Summary: Charlie Bumpers is sure he does not stand a chance of getting along with his fourth grade teacher and despite his best efforts to be neat and well-behaved, he always seems to be in trouble until he discovers her secret.
  ISBN: 978-1-56145-732-8 / 1-56145-732-9
  [1. Teachers—Fiction. 2. Schools—Fiction. 3. Orderliness—Fiction. 4. Behavior—Fiction. 5. Family life—Fiction. 6. Humorous stories.] I. Gustavson, Adam, illustrator. II. Title. III. Title: Charlie Bumpers versus the Teacher of the Year.
  PZ7.H22655Ch 2013
  [Fic]—dc23
                              2013004850

To my brothers John and Chris Harley,
from the one in the middle

It's hard to believe the great number of good people who had a hand in bringing this book from idea to the page. It's also hard to know where their suggestions end and my work begins. Thanks to all, but to these in particular: Ann Hoppe, whose idea it was; Kendra Marcus, who nursed it along; faithful readers Connie Rockman, Carol Birch, and Mary Gay Ducey; Nicole Geiger, who embraced it; Margaret Quinlin and everyone at Peachtree; Vicky Holifield, editor with the keen eye and gentle prodding; Michele Eaton; Linda and Irshad Haque, for providing a place to write in beautiful Ojai; and Debbie Block for believing in Charlie all along even when that wasn't his name.

Contents

1

Disaster Boy

My dad always says, "Charlie Bumpers, your closet looks like a tornado came through and decided to live there."

Ha ha ha. My dad is a riot. But he's right. My closet is usually a mess. And the top drawer of my dresser. And my backpack.

I mean to keep things neat. But then something else happens.

I had a couple of hours to do the impossible. My mom told me that I had put it off long enough. I had to clean out my closet before she got back… or else.

I didn't ask what she meant when she said "or else." And I didn't want to find out.

I'd already pulled out a bunch of clothes (like the sweatshirt with the Martian on it I'd thought was lost), a can of tennis balls, a Nerf football, seven socks (none of them matched), the Christmas card from Uncle Ron from when I was five (with the money taken out), two pairs of smelly old sneakers, and the dorky dress shoes I'd told Mom I couldn't find so I wouldn't have to wear them.

Then I found my old soccer ball. The little one I got when I was five. Playing soccer's my favorite thing to do. It's a lot more fun than cleaning closets.

I decided to give the old soccer ball to my little sister. She'd like it. When she likes something she squeals, and it's pretty funny.

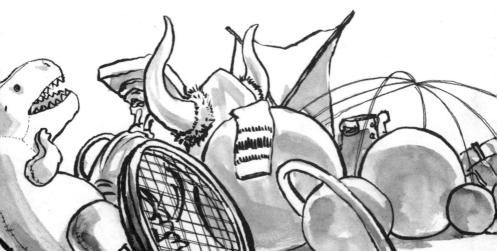

But I still wasn't done with my closet. I held my breath and went back in. I was down to the second layer.

I dragged out my second-grade project on the solar system (now missing the planets Mercury and Neptune), the ancient tennis racket my dad said I could have, a Wiffle ball bat with a crack in the handle, my Dracula costume from last Halloween, a tyrannosaurus (stuffed) and a triceratops (plastic), a bunch of busted handheld games, three trophies from teams I'd been on, a broken kite, and...

Never mind. You get the picture.

I took the Wiffle ball bat and scraped everything else out of the floor of the closet. I had to get this job done before Mom got home.

My brother Matt stuck his head in my room. "You are so dead," he said.

"What do you mean?" I asked.

"Your closet looks better, but now your room is a huge mess. Mom'll freak out!"

I looked around. Everything that had been in my closet was now scattered all over the floor. "Where am I going to put all this stuff?" I moaned.

"That's *your* problem," Matt said. "And it's a big one." Then he pulled his head out of the doorway and disappeared down the hall.

"Thanks a lot!" I yelled. "Couldn't you help me?"

"You're way beyond help," he called back. "Good luck, Disaster Boy."

Matt is two years older than me. "Two years older, two years smarter," he says.

Matt will always be older than I am, but I have hopes that someday I'll be bigger than he is and pay him back by giving him the giant noogie he truly deserves.

I had almost finished hanging up my pants and shirts when I heard Ginger's special bark that meant a car had just pulled into our driveway.

Mom! Pretty soon she'd be coming up to inspect

my closet. I panicked and started shoving stuff under my bed.

"It's me, Mabel!" my little sister yelled up the stairs, as if I wouldn't recognize her earsplitting voice. "We're home!" she squealed.

"Hey!" I yelled back. "You want my old soccer ball?"

"Charlie!" my mother called up the stairs. She sounded excited. "Guess what? I found out who your teacher is going to be!"

"What?" I stopped stuffing sweatshirts behind my beanbag chair. I didn't care if things were a mess anymore. "You know who my teacher is?"

"You have Mrs. Burke!" she shouted. "Isn't that great? Last year she was Teacher of the Year!"

My heart stopped beating for a minute, then started up again really fast, like it was trying to jump out of my chest.

It couldn't be true. There was no way I could have Mrs. Burke.

Matt was right. I was so dead.

2

Stupid Sneakers

My stomach was turning over, but I still needed to finish cleaning my room before Mom came to inspect. Or at least get everything under the bed so she wouldn't see it. I gathered up a bunch of pencils lying on the floor and opened the drawer of my desk to put them away.

The drawer was a mess, too. When I was pushing things back to make room for the pencils, I saw the old markers I'd used last year.

Maybe it would've been better if I'd stayed in third grade.

Getting Mrs. Burke for the fourth grade was the worst thing that could have happened to me. First of all, she's a neat freak. Matt didn't have Mrs. Burke for fourth grade, but he told me the kids in her class always talked about her. Everything and everyone in her class has to be really super neat and organized. Neat desks, neat notebooks, neat homework. Everything.

It was hard enough for me last year with Mr. Romano. He's one of the school's nicest teachers, and even he always said my desk was a wreck. I was sure I wouldn't last a day in Mrs. Burke's class.

Second of all, she's really tall, so she can see everything. Her head is up so high it's like a lookout tower—she can spot a kid horsing around anywhere on the playground or in the cafeteria in two seconds flat. And when she catches you doing something she doesn't like, she has this scary way of snapping her fingers at you, *POW,* like a firecracker going off.

But the biggest reason I absolutely could not have Mrs. Burke as my fourth-grade teacher was this:

SHE HATES ME!

Something happened one day last year—a *complete* accident—and ever since then Mrs. Burke has been watching me like a hawk. A hungry hawk, looking for a mouse to eat. And I was the mouse.

There was only one way to save my life. I had to get out of Mrs. Burke's class. I didn't care if she was Teacher of the Century. I knew that sometimes kids transferred to other classes. That's what I needed to do.

Maybe I could get moved to Mrs. Ladislavski's class. Everyone calls her Mrs. L. because her last name is so hard to pronounce. She's funny and friendly. That's who Matt had for fourth grade, and he says she's the best teacher in the school.

Or maybe Ms. Lewis, who was new last year and brought her dog to school one day and it threw up on Mrs. Rotelli's rug. Mrs. Rotelli is our principal. You'd think a teacher would've lost her job when her dog threw up on the principal's rug, but she didn't.

I'd even be happy to have our school custodian Mr. Turchin for fourth grade.

Anyone but Mrs. Burke.

I was thinking all these things when my mom came in my room. She walked over and looked at my closet.

"Good job, Charlie," she said. "You see? You can keep things neat."

I just nodded and hoped she wouldn't look under the bed.

"You're going to have a great school year," she said.

Mom was wrong. She didn't know about Mrs. Burke.

◆ ◆ ◆

On Saturday, Mom took the three of us to the mall to buy new clothes and school supplies. I knew this was probably my last chance to try and save my life.

Matt was in the front seat. I was in the backseat with the Squid. My dad calls her "Squirt," but I think "Squid" is funnier.

"Mom," I asked from the backseat in my best

polite voice, "can you please call Mrs. Rotelli and ask her to transfer me to another class?"

"What?" She frowned and gave me a look in the rearview mirror.

"You know, switch me to another class."

"I know what 'transfer' means, Charlie. Why on earth would you ask me to do that?"

"Because I really really need you to," I said.

"Don't be ridiculous, Charlie," she said.

"I'm not being ridiculous. I can't have Mrs. Burke. I'll die if I have her."

"No one has ever died because of who their fourth-grade teacher was," Mom said.

"Charlie might." Matt smiled back at me from the front seat. If I could have reached him without taking off my seat belt, I would have punched him. I'm glad I didn't, though. If I had, he might have told Mom the real reason I didn't want Mrs. Burke.

"Why do you think you'll die?" Mom asked.

11

"Um…I…well, I think I might be allergic to her."

"You can't be allergic to a person," the Squid said, like she was some sort of expert on the topic.

"It might be her perfume or something," I said. "She smells horrible and I'll choke to death if I have to be in her class."

"I doubt that very much," Mom said.

"Mom, please," I begged.

"I'm not calling your principal just because you didn't get the teacher you want. Anyway, you haven't even met her yet."

"I have, too," I said. "I saw her in the cafeteria and the halls all the time last year. She's really scary. When she snaps her fingers, it sounds just like fire-crackers going off."

Matt was grinning back at me, but at least he was keeping his mouth shut.

"Don't worry, Charlie," my mom said as she turned into the mall parking lot. "When you get to know her, things will be fine. I think you're lucky to have her. After all, she was Teacher of the Year."

"Dictator of the Year," I mumbled.

Matt butted in. "You'll have to be in a play, Charlie. Her class does one every year. You'll probably have to be a bunny or something."

"I don't want to be a bunny," I said. "I don't want to be in a dumb play."

"I'd love to be a bunny," the Squid said.

"Okay, okay. That's enough about Mrs. Burke," Mom said as we climbed out of the car. "Let's go get our shopping done—and I don't want any arguing like last year."

I didn't say anything else because moms don't understand, little sisters don't know, and big brothers

are bozos. I find the word "bozo" very useful when I have to describe someone. Like my brother Matt. Who is a bozo.

◆ ◆ ◆

"I'm sorry, but we're out of this style in black," the man in the shoe store said, holding out a box. "But we have your size in white."

I had picked out some really cool black sneakers with red soles that were on display in the window. "No thanks," I said. "I only want the black ones."

"Charlie, these are the exact same kind but they're white," Mom said.

I could see they were white. "I know, but I want the black ones," I said.

Mom shook her head. "We've looked

all over this mall for shoes for you and these are going to have to do. You had white ones last year and they were fine."

"No, they weren't," I said. But Mom paid the man, handed me the shoe bag, and herded us all toward the mall exit.

All I could think about were my best friend Tommy's great new sneakers. They were all black, even the laces.

On the way back to the car, my sister chanted in a voice low enough that Mom couldn't hear, "I got blue shoes, I got blue shoes…"

"Mom," I said when we got in the car, "can't we try another mall? I really wanted black ones like Tommy's. I hate white sneakers. They're so stupid."

"Please don't use that word." Mom hates it when we say "stupid."

Sometimes, though, stupid is the only word that fits. Like when you're talking about stupid white sneakers.

Mom pulled out of the parking lot.

"I don't blame you, Charlie," Matt said. "White sneakers are dorky. Everyone is going to make fun of you."

"Matt, stop it," Mom said.

Matt shrugged. "Okay. But I really do feel bad for Charlie. Those sneakers are just about the dorkiest—"

"Shut up!" I said.

"Charlie!" Mom was using her I-mean-it voice. We aren't supposed to say "shut up," either.

Matt twisted around so Mom couldn't see his face and gave me his evil older brother smile. "Too bad I'll be in middle school this year," he said. "I won't be there to protect you when people make fun of your shoes."

I stared at him and mouthed the words, *Shut up, stupid.* Then I gave up and stared out the side window.

In a way, Matt was right. It was too bad he wouldn't be at my school anymore. Even though he bugged me at home until I wanted to scream, he'd always looked after me on the bus or in the hallways at school. And his friends would always wave and say hi to me. Now none of them would be at King Philip Elementary.

I would be stuck there alone with Mrs. Burke.

And my stupid white sneakers.

3
What a Bozo!

By the time we got home from shopping, I was mad at everyone and everything.

I took my new clothes into my room and threw them on my bed. I pulled out the shoebox and opened the lid a crack, hoping that maybe the clerk had been wrong and had miraculously found a black pair in my size.

Boogers! The shoes were still white. They were blindingly white. Disgustingly white. Horribly white.

I hated those stupid sneakers. Maybe my old sneakers would be okay to wear. At least they weren't snow-white anymore.

I got down on the floor and searched under my bed. It took me a long time to find them because they were buried under all the stuff I'd cleaned out of my closet. But the moment I pulled them out, I realized that I couldn't wear them this year.

These were the shoes that had made Mrs. Burke hate me in the first place!

I stuffed them back under the bed.

I pulled the new sneakers out of their box again and looked at them.

They were the right kind, but the wrong color. And then it hit me. Why do they have to *stay* this color? One time my mom hadn't liked the color of a pair of her shoes, so she'd dyed them.

Why couldn't I do that?

I got my black marker and colored a little spot on the back of the heel of one of the sneakers.

It looked pretty good! I colored a little more on the side.

It still looked pretty good.

Pretty soon, half the sneaker was black.

Now it didn't look so good.

But there was no turning back. I had to color the whole shoe.

Then my marker ran out.

I looked all over the house and finally found another one in the jar on my mom's desk. When I'd colored in the top of the second sneaker, I realized that the new marker looked like a different shade of black, sort of a really dark gray. Who knew that there were different colors of *black*? But I kept going until I had covered the entire shoe.

I even colored the shoelaces, which took a long time. I didn't color the bottoms, since they were already red.

I put the shoes on. Then I took them off.

They didn't look like stupid white sneakers anymore.

They looked like stupid black sneakers.

What a bozo!

20

4
Maybe There Was a Mistake?

I woke up on the first day of school feeling queasy. I'd been going to King Philip Elementary School forever, so I guess I shouldn't have been nervous about the first day anymore. But I was. Even though it was the same old school, things were different.

Like knowing that I was going to have Mrs. Burke—and *not* knowing who was going to be in my class.

When I got dressed and put on my new sneakers, I realized Mom wasn't going to like what I'd done. I hoped she wouldn't notice.

Lucky for me, the first day of school was a big deal for my little sister, and she kept asking Mom for help getting ready. My brother and my dad left before I went down for breakfast. I thought I was safe.

Then, Mom noticed.

"What on earth did you do to your sneakers?" she asked.

Trick question! I knew there was no good answer.

"I don't know," I said, which is a good thing to say when adults ask trick questions.

"Oh, Charlie, why did you do that?"

"I wanted black ones," I said.

She shook her head and started clearing away the breakfast dishes. She was slamming things around a little, so I knew she was mad.

On the bus, the Squid wanted to sit with me. "Why don't you sit there and save a seat for Carla?" I said. "I'll be right here behind you in the next row sitting with Tommy. They get on in two stops."

"Okay," she said, sliding into the seat in front of me. "I can't wait to see Mrs. Dizzaz."

"You mean Di-az," I corrected her. Mrs. Diaz had been my teacher in first grade, and now the Squid was in her class.

She looked at me like I was making a joke or

something. "That's what I said—Dizzaz."

I gave up and sat down. I couldn't wait to see Tommy. He and I have been best friends since second grade. He is excellent at many things. He draws great cartoons. He can make his voice sound just like a sports announcer. He does a hilarious duck imitation. He can turn his eyelids inside out and it's really gross and none of the grown-ups can stand it. But he also has a habit of blurting things out when it would be better to keep his mouth shut. Like the time he told my dad that we didn't mean to let the air out of the car tire.

Tommy and his little sister Carla got on.

"Hey, Charlie," he said. "Guess what?"

"What?"

"I know who I have for a teacher," he said.

"Me too." I suddenly got a really sick feeling because something occurred to me. We had always been in the same class. What if Tommy didn't have Mrs. Burke?

"Who do you have?" he asked.

"You first," I said.

"I got Mrs. L. Did you?"

I looked down at the floor. The engine roared and the bus bounced up and down. My stomach tied itself in a knot. I shook my head.

"No? You didn't? Are you sure?"

I nodded. Now, even worse, I felt tears filling up my eyes. I didn't want to cry so I looked out the window.

"Who'd you get?"

I gave Tommy a don't-ask look. He slapped his hand over his mouth— he could tell just from the look on my face.

"Not...not Mrs. Burke?" he said.

I nodded again.

Tommy shook his head. "I can't believe it."

"Neither can I."

"Maybe you can switch teachers?"

"I already asked my mom and she said that was ridiculous. I told her that I was allergic to Mrs. Burke but it didn't do any good."

"Did you tell your mom what happened?"

"No!" I said. "Do you think I'm crazy?"

"Well, yes," he said. "That's why we're friends."

That made me laugh, even though I knew I was going to die as soon as I got to school.

Then Tommy looked down and saw my sneakers. "Wow," he said, "what happened to your shoes?"

"I don't want to talk about it," I said. "All I can say is they didn't have the black ones like yours, so I made some adjustments."

"Oh," Tommy said. Then he added, "They don't look *that* bad."

"Thanks," I said, but I knew Tommy was just trying to make me feel better. That's what best friends are for—when you do something that makes you look like a bozo, they tell you it isn't that bad.

Neither of us said anything for a minute. I wondered if you could still be best friends if you weren't in the same class. Then I thought maybe his mom would let him change to Mrs. Burke's class, even though then we'd both be miserable. But at least we'd be miserable together, which is a lot better than being miserable alone.

"Maybe it'll be okay," Tommy said. "She was Teacher of the Year last year."

"I think grown-ups give that award," I said. "I know I didn't vote for her."

"Neither did I," Tommy agreed. "But maybe she's forgotten what happened."

"Yeah, right. No way."

"I know," he said. "I was just trying to help."

How could she possibly forget? I was so dead.

"But it was sort of funny," Tommy said. "When you think about it."

I thought about it.

◆ ◆ ◆

Mr. Romano was the best third-grade teacher. Every Friday afternoon at the end of the day he would let us play games in class.

Once when Tommy and I were partners for Mystery Word, we had to go out in the hall while we waited for the class to decide on a secret word for us to figure out.

It took them a long time to decide, and we started messing around.

Tommy stepped on the back of my sneaker and pulled it off. Then he wouldn't give it back.

I wrestled him to the floor and pulled off one of his sneakers.

We were both laughing.

Then he threw my shoe down the hall.

I threw his shoe, too.

Just as I let go, a teacher came out of her classroom.

And…the sneaker hit her in the head.

It was a complete accident. I would *never* hit a teacher in the head with a sneaker on purpose.

Guess who the teacher was?

Right. Mrs. Burke.

She was pretty surprised. I can see how anyone who got hit in the head by a sneaker in the school hallway would be surprised. Sneakers don't usually fly down the hallways of schools.

She was also pretty mad. She picked up the flying shoe. Then she saw my shoe that Tommy had thrown and picked it up, too. She walked toward us. "Who threw this?" she growled, holding up Tommy's shoe. I guess she didn't ask about my shoe since it hadn't hit her in the head.

"I did," I said. I wondered if she was going to beat me with Tommy's shoe.

"I threw the other one," Tommy confessed. He didn't have to say that. It sure didn't help things much.

Because then she said the words I'll never forget: *"If I ever see you throw another shoe in school, you will stay in from recess for the rest of your life!"*

The rest of your life is a very long time.

Especially if you're eight years old, which I was at the time. If you lived to be a hundred, that would be ninety-two years without recess.

Then Mr. Romano came out of the classroom and Mrs. Burke told him what had happened and he took our shoes and gave them back to us and told us to sit down. We didn't get to play Mystery Word anymore.

Mr. Romano didn't say a word to us.

That's how he usually was when he got mad. Sometimes when adults don't say anything it's worse than when they yell.

It was a bad day.

But I learned an important lesson that afternoon:

NEVER, EVER HIT A TEACHER IN THE HEAD WITH A SNEAKER. ESPECIALLY THE TEACHER OF THE YEAR.

◆ ◆ ◆

"Well, it isn't funny to me," I told Tommy, "now that I have Mrs. Burke for a teacher."

Carla and the Squid, Tommy, and I got off the bus together at school and walked in through the front door. Mrs. Rotelli, the principal, and Mrs. Finch, the school secretary, were greeting everyone and telling them where to find their classrooms.

I already knew where mine was. Mrs. Burke's prison.

There was also a lady to show the first graders to their classes. She took Carla and the Squid by their hands and led them down the hall.

"Hi, Mrs. Rotelli," Tommy blurted out. "I think maybe there was a mistake. Charlie and I have always been in the same class together, and I'm pretty sure he couldn't have Mrs. Burke. Can you check and see?"

Mrs. Rotelli stared at him for a second, then looked down at the clipboard. "He does have Mrs. Burke. Is there some reason he shouldn't?"

Tommy glanced over at me.

I rolled my eyes. Why couldn't he keep his mouth shut?

"Um, no," he said.

"Then I hope you have a good school year. Both of you boys can head to your classrooms."

5

Surrounded

Mrs. Burke was standing outside her door. She was tall and her face was long. She looked like an egret—a bird with long legs that catches fish in the water.

I was the fish.

Her glasses had bright orange frames. Her eyes were looking right at me. I tried not to look back.

When I got to the door, I gave her a quick smile and tried to slip by.

She caught my arm with her bony fingers. Her bony firecracker-exploding fingers!

I didn't mean to scream, but I did.

"AAAAAAAAAAAH!"

She let go of my arm and squinted at me. Her glasses fell off her nose and swung from the chain around her neck. "What's wrong?" she asked. "What happened?"

"Um...nothing," I said.

"Mr. Bumpers," she said, "you walked in here like you were headed to prison."

"Ummm...I...I...," I stammered.

"Welcome to Mrs. Burke's top-security penitentiary," she said with an evil smile.

I looked at her. I'd never heard that word.

"Penitentiary means prison," she said.

I knew it! And I was going to be locked up here for a whole year!

She looked down at the papers she was holding. I could see that the one on top was a seating chart.

I hate seating charts.

"Let's see where your *cell* is going to be," she said, squeezing my shoulder with her exploding fingers so I couldn't escape.

"Ah, yes. I know all about you, Charlie Bumpers. I have a special place for you. You're in the third seat in the second row."

I nodded and started to walk toward my desk.

"Charlie," she said to me.

I turned back.

She was looking at my feet.

"I'm glad to see you're wearing both of your shoes."

◆ ◆ ◆

Alex McLeod was sitting in the front of the class. He was already having trouble staying in his seat. Mr. Romano used to say that Alex had "crazy legs" and that they had to move constantly or they would fall off.

One of his crazy legs stuck out and nearly tripped me.

"Charlie!" Alex said. "Where are you sitting? By me?"

"No," I said. "Back there." I walked down the aisle and sat in my seat. I put my new stuff in my desk very carefully.

Last year I got good grades on my final report card, but at the bottom Mr. Romano wrote that I had a hard time being organized. I remember his exact words:

Next year, Charlie should work harder on keeping things neat and orderly. This will make life easier for him and everyone else around him. I know he can do it.

My parents had read that to me. Three times.

I put the plastic pen and pencil holder in one corner of my desk and the big binder in the other. I put the scissors and notepads down near the bottom, right in the exact center.

Everything was perfect.

"Hi, Charlie," Ellen Holmes said, sliding into the desk just in front of mine.

"Hi, Ellen," I said. I was glad she was in front

of me. Ellen is funny and kind of smart, and she spends most of her time drawing horses. She collects little plastic horse models and has a million books about horses. Last year she kept one of her horse books on her lap and read it while everyone else was doing math.

Josh Little sat at the desk on my right. One day in second grade, in front of the whole school, Mrs. Rotelli used him as an example of someone who was polite. I felt sorry for him. No one wants a principal to point out how polite you are in front of everybody.

Then a kid I'd never seen before sat on my left.

"Hi," I said. "My name's Charlie. Are you new?"

He just nodded.

He was wearing glasses with black frames and his clothes were all new. His shirt was tucked into his pants. He looked very neat, like someone who would take a bath without being told.

His sneakers were new, too.

They were exactly like mine.

Except he hadn't colored them with a marker and they were still white.

"What's your name?" I asked.

He said something that sounded like "Achetore." He held up his notebook and pointed to his name printed in big letters on the front.

"Oh," I said. "Hi, Hector."

He gave me a little wave and looked back down. He seemed kind of shy. "I just moved here," he said, without exactly looking at me. He just kept staring down at the stuff in his desk.

I decided not to tell him he would've been better off staying wherever he was before.

Far from Mrs. Burke.

"Good luck," I said, nodding toward her desk. "We're all going to need it."

His face broke out into a big smile, and then he covered his mouth with his hand like he was smiling too much and his face might fall off.

I leaned over and whispered to him, "Watch out for Mrs. Burke."

He shrugged. "It's okay."

That's what he thinks, I said to myself. But then, he did look like the kind of kid who always did what he was supposed to do. He'd probably never have to stay in from recess.

When Hector finished organizing the things in his desk, he just sat there, not saying anything.

He's not messy, I thought. *And I'll bet he's smart, too.*

Now all the desks in my corner were taken, except the one right behind me. I wished Tommy was in my class and that was his seat.

I heard a loud voice at the front of the room.

Samantha Grunsky.

Boogers!

Samantha Grunsky has been in my class every year. She's the kind of kid who always reminds you how smart she is. She drives me crazy.

Last year in social studies I did my report on the rainforest. I spent a lot of time making a rainforest in a terrarium. I worked on it for a whole month.

Samantha Grunsky did the rainforest, too. But

her parents ordered actual rainforest plants for her and she typed out this really long report herself. When we brought our reports in, she pointed out to Mr. Romano that I had spelled "arboreal" and "nocturnal" wrong on my poster.

Samantha Grunsky is a bozo. Even if she is smart.

She turned down my aisle and walked toward me. "Oh, no," she said. "Look who I'm sitting behind."

"Oh no," I said. "Look who I'm sitting in front of."

She crossed her eyes at me. "I'm sure Mrs. Burke made a mistake giving me this seat. Once she gets to know me, she'll see that I should be in a seat near the front so she can call on me easier."

I looked at everyone around me, and then I looked at Mrs. Burke. I remembered what she'd said to me when I came in: *I know about you.*

Right then I realized what Mrs. Burke was doing. She had surrounded me with kids who were really neat and behaved all the time and always did what they were supposed to do, because she wanted me to be neat and good, too.

Hector the New Kid was probably put there because he didn't talk much and never did anything wrong. I looked over at him. He was staring at my shoes.

I wondered if I was going to have to throw one at him to make him stop gawking at them.

This was going to be a long, long year.

6

Does Anyone Know Where Chile Is?

Alex McLeod was almost destroyed by Mrs. Burke's exploding fingers that morning.

We were doing math problems at our desks and he got up and started talking to Dashawn Tremont.

"Alex!" Mrs. Burke called out. *POW! POW! POW!* Her finger snaps echoed across the room.

Everyone looked up.

The snaps worked like magic. Alex ran back over to his seat and started writing like a maniac.

"Listen, class," our teacher said. "Rule number one in Mrs. Burke's empire: Stay at your desk unless you have permission to get up."

Empire! She called it her empire? I knew it. She was a dictator and we were her slaves!

Right before lunch, Mrs. Burke had the new kids

in class introduce themselves. There were three in all: Hector, a girl named Candy Carlofsky, and a boy named Trevor David. First, Mrs. Burke asked Candy to stand up and tell the class where she'd moved from and if she had any brothers or sisters or pets. Then she did the same for Trevor.

It was Hector's turn to talk next. He was looking down at his desk. His right knee was jiggling like mine does sometimes when I'm in the doctor's office waiting for a shot.

"Class," said Mrs. Burke. "I have a question for you. Anyone but Hector may answer it."

Everyone looked at Hector. His ears were turning red around the edges. He took off his glasses and wiped them off with a little cloth.

"Does anyone know where Chile is?" Mrs. Burke asked.

I thought of something hilarious and raised my hand before Samantha could get hers in the air.

"Yes, Charlie?" Mrs. Burke said.

"It's where it's cold. Where it's chilly all the time."

Alex and some of the other kids laughed.

Mrs. Burke didn't even crack a smile. She gave me a big frown and shook her head.

Samantha Grunsky was waving her hand like a big smelly flag or something.

"Yes, Samantha," Mrs. Burke said.

"It's in South America," said Samantha. "It's a long, skinny country and it has mountains called the Andes."

Mrs. Burke smiled. "Very good, Samantha."

I turned and looked at her. "Very good, genius," I muttered, wagging my head and screwing up my face.

"What you said was dumb," she whispered.

"Not as dumb as you," I hissed back.

POW! POW! Mrs. Burke's fingers exploded again. Everybody got quiet. "Rule number two in my empire: We will all show respect to our neighbors." She looked down at the notebook on her desk. "It just so happens that Hector and his family are from Chile. Isn't that right, Hector?"

Hector the New Kid barely looked up.

I guess what I said *had* been dumb. I'd made fun of his country by mistake. Now I was the bozo.

"Hector, can you tell us why you moved here to the United States?" Mrs. Burke asked.

Then Hector the New Kid did a weird thing. He stood up by his desk to give his answer. Maybe that's how they do it in Chile. He spoke in a voice so soft some kids on the other side of the room probably couldn't hear him. He was looking down at the floor while he spoke.

"My father is a businessman. His company asked him to work here in the United States," he said with his Chile accent. "We are living here for three years."

A couple of kids giggled. I was starting to feel sorry for Hector the New Kid. All he did was answer the question, and kids were laughing at him.

"Thank you, Hector," Mrs. Burke said. "You may sit down now." Hector sat, but Mrs. Burke wasn't done with him. "Maybe you can help us this year," she went on. "We're going to be studying Spanish. A language teacher will be coming to our class twice a week."

She smiled at him, and then she glared at me like she was warning me not to be a bozo again.

She told Hector that there were some other kids in our class who could speak Spanish already, like Joey Alvarez and Carmen Torres. Their families had moved here from Mexico and the Dominican Republic a long time ago. I think Mrs. Burke was trying to make him feel comfortable.

"I already know some Spanish," said Samantha Grunsky.

That figures, I thought. *She always has to already know everything.*

"*Buenos días*," Samantha said in a loud voice, so everyone could hear how smart she was.

Hector looked like he was going to throw up. I couldn't blame him. I figured kids threw up in Chile, too.

"*Buenos días*," he said back to Samantha.

"Very good," said Mrs. Burke. She was beaming. She was probably congratulating herself on doing such a good job keeping Charlie Bumpers in line, surrounding him with kids who were always good and could speak other languages.

And I was supposed to learn from them.

I would *never* learn from Samantha Grunsky.

I would rather be a bozo.

When we lined up to go to lunch, Hector the New Kid was behind me. Right before we walked down the hall he asked, "Did you color those shoes yourself?"

I nodded.

"With a marker?"

"It took two," I said. "It was a dumb idea."

He just shrugged. He was too polite to say how dumb it was.

I looked at his clean white shoes. They didn't look *that* bad.

7

Supreme Commander of Soccer Balls

After lunch, we were about to go outside for recess when Mrs. Burke said, "Charlie?"

"Yes?" I answered. I knew from her tone of voice that something was wrong.

"Is that your desk with all the things still on it?"

I looked across the room. I had left my math folder out and some pencils. And an eraser. And a ruler.

"Yes," I said.

"Please clean them up," she said. "We'll wait for you."

I hurried across the room and stuffed the folder and pencils and eraser into the desk. It was bad enough having to waste my own recess time to pick up my things—but it was worse that everyone was staring at me and waiting to go outside.

When I got back in line, Mrs. Burke said to everyone, "Rule number three in my empire: Always remember to put things away."

Everyone nodded and looked at me.

Samantha Grunsky said, "Charlie always has a messy desk."

"Not this year," Mrs. Burke said. Then she turned and led us down the hall.

When we finally got to the playground, I couldn't find Tommy anywhere. While I was standing there looking, a little kid came up to me.

"Charlie! Charlie!" he shouted in a hoarse voice. I'd never seen him before, and I wondered how he knew my name.

"Yeah," I said. "Who are you?"

"Brady Bernhart," he said. "I'm in first grade. Will you tie my shoes?"

I looked down at his feet. Both of his shoelaces were untied and were dragging on the ground.

"Uh…sure." I knelt down and double knotted the laces like my mom taught me so they wouldn't come undone.

"Thanks, Charlie," he said in his croaky little voice.

It was strange that he hadn't asked his teacher to tie his shoes. "How come you asked me?"

He turned and pointed to where a bunch of second graders were playing. "They said you'd do it," he said. Then he ran off.

Little kids are weird.

Just then, Tommy ran up to me bouncing a brand-new soccer ball.

"Hey, Charlie. How's Mrs. Burke?" he asked.

"Worse than I thought," I said. "She's already shot Alex with her exploding fingers."

Tommy groaned. "Poor Alex."

"And I said something stupid

about where this new kid Hector is from and Mrs. Burke frowned at me and then she made me clean up my desk while the whole class waited to go outside for recess. I'm doomed."

"It sounds like it."

"But here's the worst part—she put me in a seat right in front of Samantha Grunsky!"

"Oh no!" he said. Then he laughed and tossed the soccer ball up in the air. "Guess who's in front of me."

"Who?"

"Darren Thompson. And he's even bigger than he was last year."

"Uh-oh," I said.

Darren Thompson is the kind of kid who's acting all friendly one minute, and the next minute he's giving you a wedgie, which is what he did to me when we were in second grade.

He pulled on my underwear waistband so hard that it totally stretched out. I could barely fit it back into my pants. I never wore that underwear again.

"You've got to watch out for him," I said. Tommy threw me the soccer ball. It was shiny and new, white with blue spots.

"Hey, where'd you get this?" I asked him.

"Found it in the gym," he said. "The new gym teacher must have ordered new ones this year. You want to play a game?"

We found some other kids and chose up sides and started to play. It was a close game. After my team scored its second goal, I noticed Hector the New Kid standing off to the side, watching.

"You want to play?" I called out, waving at him.

He just shrugged his shoulders and didn't say anything.

"Hey, wait a minute!" I called to my team. "Hector wants to play!"

Everyone stopped and stared at me.

No one knew who Hector was.

"He can't," Sam Marchand said. "The teams won't be even."

I looked at Hector the New Kid. He shrugged again, like he didn't care. But I could tell that he did, and I felt kind of bad for him. It wasn't his fault he was new and no one knew him.

"No problem," I told Sam. "He can play for me." I turned to Hector and pointed down the field. "You're on the team shooting at that goal."

"It's okay," he said. "I don't have to—"

"Go ahead," I said. "I don't mind. There's just a little time left."

Hector the New Kid took off his glasses and put them in his pocket, then ran out onto the field. I stood on the sideline and watched. The ball went back and forth, up and down the field, but no one scored. Kids passed the ball to their friends, but no one passed the ball to Hector.

I guess they hadn't noticed what I had.

Hector the New Kid was really fast. Whenever

there was someone chasing the ball, Hector got to it first. Then he would pass it right away to a kid on his team.

When it was almost time to go in, someone kicked the ball out of bounds right to me, so I caught it.

"Hey, look," said Sam, pointing toward the gym. "It must be the new gym teacher."

A man in a dark blue warm-up suit was marching out onto the field. Mrs. Burke was with him. When they reached us, the man blew his whistle.

"Everyone over here!" Mrs. Burke called.

We all ran over. The man stood there with his arms folded like he was a general in the army. I was holding the new soccer ball. It wasn't quite as white and shiny as it was before.

The man stared at me. "May I have that, please?" he asked.

I handed it to him.

He put it under his arm without saying thank you. "Listen up, fourth graders," he said. "I'm Mr. Shuler. Gym equipment needs to stay in the gym."

"We needed a soccer ball," said Tommy. "Mr. Collins always let us borrow them."

"Mr. Collins isn't here anymore. I'm your new physical education teacher, and I'd like to keep track of the new equipment. Before you borrow a ball, you'll need to ask permission from me. You have other equipment for the playground."

Tommy said, "Yeah, but—"

Mr. Shuler held up his finger for Tommy to be quiet. It was a big finger. At the end of a big arm. On a big body. "Excuse me," he said.

We all stood there. Most kids looked down at the ground. Mr. Shuler wasn't anything like Mr. Collins.

"No use of gym equipment without permission," he said. "Does everyone understand?"

We all nodded.

"Okay," he said. "I'll look forward to seeing you in class."

We nodded again. There was nothing to say to a new gym teacher who didn't let you play with the new soccer balls.

"Let's line up," said Mrs. Burke. "It's time to go in."

"Why can't we use the soccer ball?" I asked her after Mr. Shuler went back into the school building.

"Mr. Shuler is just doing his job," she said.

If his job is keeping soccer balls away from us so we can't have fun, I thought, *he's really good at it.*

Right then and there, I gave Mr. Shuler a new name: General Shuler, Intergalactic Supreme Commander of Soccer Balls.

8

A Colossal Mistake

Our family eats dinner together almost every night. Some evenings my dad has to work late. Sometimes my mom, who is a visiting nurse, has to be away at dinnertime. But mostly, we eat together.

And every weeknight, Dad makes us give reports on our school day. If you don't say enough, he makes everyone else be quiet until you say more. He doesn't care what you tell about. You can make up something silly if you want. Once I said, "Today the entire third grade threw up from eating moldy chicken fingers." My dad laughed. He's a pretty funny guy, and he likes it when we make jokes.

But that night I didn't feel like being funny. For one thing, Mrs. Burke had given our class more homework than I'd ever had before.

"You first, Squirt," Dad said to my sister.

She talked for a million hours. It took her longer to talk about her day than the day itself. At the end, she looked straight at me and said, "And her name is Mrs. *Diaz*, not Dizzaz."

"I told you that," I said.

"No, you didn't," she said.

Dad asked my brother to go next. Usually he asked me second, but I think he could tell I wasn't in a talking mood. I was busy scowling at the Squid.

My brother had plenty to say about his first day

at middle school. "We go to different rooms for different classes. We have to carry around a map of the school so we won't get lost. Jason's in all my classes but one. It's really cool, and at lunch you can sit anywhere you want."

That made me even grumpier. If Mrs. Burke was in charge of the middle school, they'd probably have to sit in assigned seats even at lunch.

Then my father looked at me.

"Well, Charlie, I see you're still breathing after your first day."

"Too bad," said Matt.

"Matt," Mom said.

"I have a whole hour of homework tonight," I grumbled.

"I don't have any homework," said the Squid. "I want homework."

"You can have mine," said Matt.

"You don't usually complain about homework, Charlie," my father said. "Is something else wrong?"

"Mrs. Burke has a million rules."

"Wow," said Dad. "That's a lot of rules! Does she write them all up on the board, or do you have to memorize them?"

Sometimes when my dad's being funny, it isn't funny. I ignored him.

"And we have to sit in assigned places," I added.

Dad just gave me a look. He still didn't seem to feel very bad for me.

"And Samantha Grunsky sits right behind me."

"Uh-oh. I seem to remember you talking about her," Dad said and took a bite of potatoes.

"You know, Dad," Matt said, "that's the girl Charlie wants to marry when he—"

"BE QUIET, YOU IDIOT!" I shouted.

"Charlie!" said my mom.

"Oh my," said Matt. "What language!"

"You're not supposed to say 'idiot,'" said the Squid.

"Hey, Mabel," said Matt. "You just said 'idiot.'"

"But not like Charlie!" she yelled. "I was just saying *not* to say it!"

"But you did say 'idiot,'" said Matt.

"You said 'idiot,' too," she said. Now she was laughing because she knew she was saying it. Everyone had forgotten that we were talking about what happened to me.

"Enough!" said my dad. "No more idiots!"

"Now *you* said it!" squealed the Squid.

They were all laughing. Ginger was barking. She always barks when people laugh, like it's her way of laughing. Everyone was laughing or barking.

Except me. I still thought Matt really was an idiot.

When the laughing died down, my mom spoke up. "Mrs. Burke can't be that bad, Charlie. Did she talk about the play you'll put on?"

"You mean when Charlie gets to be the bunny?" Matt asked.

I ignored my brother's comment.

"I'll be the bunny," the Squid said.

"Something good must have happened today at school," Mom said to me.

"Nothing I can think of. Even the new gym teacher is like an army general and won't let us use the new soccer balls. And Mrs. Burke isn't going to like me no matter what I do."

"Mrs. L. liked me right away," Matt said. "We got along great."

"Matt!" Dad said. "That's not helpful."

"I'm sure Mrs. Burke will grow to like you," Mom said.

"She hates me," I said. "I can tell by the way she looks at me."

"Everyone always likes you, Charlie. Wait until

she sees all the things you're good at."

"Like what?" I said.

"You're good at math," Mom said.

She was right. I was pretty good at math.

"And reading."

"Okay, okay," I said.

"You're good at being an idiot," said Matt.

"Stop it, Matt," Dad said. "I mean it."

"You're good at a lot of things," Mom went on. "And you're a good kid."

That's what moms do. They tell you you're good when you think you're not.

"Mom, Mrs. Burke just doesn't like me," I said. "And I'll never like her. I can't believe she was ever Teacher of the Year."

Dad put his fork down. "Charlie, you don't have to like Mrs. Burke, but you do have to learn to get along with her because you're stuck with her for the whole year."

"You mean like you're stuck with Mr. Grimaldi?" I asked.

My dad screwed up his mouth and looked at the ceiling. Mr. Grimaldi was his new boss. Dad wasn't happy when his old boss Mr. Ralston left and Mr. Grimaldi took his place. He was always complaining to Mom about him. I guess sometimes parents don't realize that their kids hear what they're saying to each other. But we do.

"Charlie," said my mom, "you shouldn't say things like that."

"I agree completely," said Matt.

"Hold it." Dad held up his hands. "That's a fair question. Yes. You're stuck with Mrs. Burke just like I'm stuck with Mr. Grimaldi."

"Do you get along with Mr. Grimaldi now?" I asked.

"I'm working on it," he said.

"Well," I said, "when you learn to get along with Mr. Grimaldi, maybe I'll learn to get along with Mrs. Burke."

It was quiet at the table. Dad looked at Mom, then back at me. He held up a finger. "Okay. I'll make you a deal. I'll learn to get along with Mr. Grimaldi if you learn to get along with Mrs. Burke. Is it a deal?"

Trick question! No good answer!

Dad stuck his hand out across the table for me to shake.

I looked at it. I didn't want to shake it, because that meant I would have to learn to get along with Mrs. Burke. But he was my dad. So I shook it.

"I already like Mrs. Diaz!" said the Squid.

"You mean Mrs. Dizzaz?" asked Matt.

"No! Diaz, Diaz, Diaz!" said the Squid.

Everyone laughed again. Ginger barked. But I didn't laugh. I knew I'd made an enormous, colossal mistake by making a deal with my dad. Because I would never be able to get along with Mrs. Burke.

I'd rather quit school and go to work and try to get along with Mr. Grimaldi.

9
The Egg is Wrong

Somehow I made it to Friday without dying.

When I got to school that morning, I saw that Mrs. Burke had hung up a sign in the hallway with these words printed on it: "Our Favorite Books."

The day before, we had drawn pictures of scenes from our favorite books. Now all the pictures were taped to a long string hanging on the wall. It looked great stretching up and down the hall.

My favorite book is *Jeremy Thatcher, Dragon Hatcher,* which I've read a million times.

Or at least three.

My picture of Jeremy Thatcher looking at the dragon egg was hanging right over our classroom door so everyone could see it when they walked in.

Jeremy Thatcher
Dragon Hatcher

by Charlie Company

Mrs. Burke was just inside the room, looking down at me. Up close she seemed even taller. "I liked your drawing very much, Charlie," she said. "Good job."

I was speechless. Mrs. Burke had said something nice. About me!

Some other kids told me they thought the picture was cool, too. Even Ellen Holmes, who can draw really good pictures, especially horses.

Then Samantha Grunsky spoke up. "Your picture's wrong," she said.

"What do you mean?" I asked.

"I read the book. The egg is rainbow colored."

Samantha was even more annoying than that girl in the book who drove Jeremy Thatcher crazy. "I don't care," I said. I had colored it gold because my favorite pencil was gold colored.

"It's still wrong," she sniffed, like she was the

Queen of Books or something.

I'd really liked the egg the way it was, but after Samantha said that, it started to bug me. Every time I walked past the door, there was my picture right overhead, with the egg the wrong color.

When we lined up for recess, Mrs. Burke put me in the front of the line right next to Samantha Grunsky.

"Your picture's still wrong," she whispered.

"So's your brain," I said.

"When everyone is through talking," Mrs. Burke said, "we can go."

We all got quiet and followed her out to the playground. I spotted Tommy standing with some other kids by the fence. It looked like they were arguing about something.

"Are you kidding?" Tommy said to Darren Thompson just as I came over. "Charlie can beat you by a mile!"

Uh-oh. If only Tommy could learn to keep his big mouth shut once in a while.

"Hey, Charlie," Tommy said. "You're still the fastest, aren't you?"

"I don't know," I muttered. I was the fastest last year at field day, but not by much. I'd barely beat out Darren. And Caitlyn Wang had almost beaten both of us. "I guess we'll find out on field day," I said.

"No contest," Darren said. "I'll beat you by a mile this year."

"No, you won't!" Tommy shouted. "Let's have a race now!"

I looked at Tommy like he was crazy. Why does he always blurt out stuff without thinking? Even if I did beat Darren, he'd probably just give me a wedgie again.

By now other kids were all chanting, "Let's have a race! Let's have a race!"

I didn't feel like racing. I couldn't stop thinking about dumb Samantha Grunsky and the wrong-colored dragon egg. "Not now," I said, heading back toward the school. "I have to do something inside."

"Chicken!" Darren said.

"That's not it!" I yelled back.

"Buck-buck-buck buck-aww!" Darren said, flapping his arms like chicken wings.

"Come on, Charlie!" Tommy pleaded. "I know you can beat him!"

I kept walking. That dragon egg picture was on my mind and I had to take care of it now.

I was almost to the door when I heard someone on the playground yelling my name.

I stopped.

Brady, the first grader with the funny voice, was running toward me. "Charlie!" He was still yelling even though he was only a few feet away. "I can't get my jacket unzipped!"

I looked around. There were teachers all over the place. But Brady just stood there staring up at me with his big eyes. I got down on my knees and unzipped his jacket.

"Wait," I said as he turned to go. "Your shoe-laces are untied again."

He glanced down at his shoes, then back at me.

I tied the laces and gave them a double knot.

"Thanks, Charlie," he said in his croaky little voice and ran off.

It's a good thing Brady's head was stuck on permanently. If it wasn't, he'd probably lose it.

I went back inside and headed down the hallway to my classroom.

10

Aaaaaaaaaaaah!

I reached up to pull down my drawing, but it was a little too high. Then I noticed a desk and chair sitting right outside Ms. Lewis's room. I dragged the chair over, climbed up onto the seat, and pulled on my drawing. Mrs. Burke had stapled it to the string. It wouldn't come off.

I jumped down and raced into our classroom to get my colored pencils. They were way in the back of my desk, so I had to take everything else out to get to them. I stuck the pencils I needed in my pocket and ran back to the chair. Everything was still quiet. Recess wouldn't be over for a few more minutes.

I stood on the chair again. I could reach the picture, but I wasn't high enough to color it. I just needed to be a few inches higher.

I looked over at the desk.

I KNOW you're not supposed to stand on a desk. I'm not a bozo.

But there was nobody around, and I figured I'd be done with standing on it and fixing the egg before anyone else came back.

It wasn't easy, but I pushed the desk in front of the door, right under my picture. I balanced myself on top, pulled the pencils from my pocket, and started to color the first rainbow stripe on the gold egg.

That was when things began to go wrong.

One leg of the desk was a little wobbly and the desk shifted under my feet. I put my hands up on the wall to balance myself, but I hit the string holding up the pictures.

The tape holding one end of the string came loose and the pictures began to fall. I tried to hold them up, but they flapped and fluttered and the string fell across my shoulders. I still had the colored pencils in one hand, so I tried to hold up the string of pictures with my other hand.

Then the other end of the string came loose. Pictures were wrapping around me. I couldn't see.

My foot slipped off the edge of the desk.

I reached out for anything to keep me from falling and got one hand on the top of the door. It started to swing away from me, so I grabbed hold with the other hand, too. The door swung around until it hit the wall.

There I was, hanging on the door with all the pictures the class had drawn of their favorite books strangling me and stretching down the hallway.

"Help!" I squeaked, hoping someone could hear me.

Then the door started to swing back toward the doorframe. My fingers were going to be smashed!

Just in time, I kicked at the wall and the door went flying back the other way. When it slammed against the hallway wall, the board on the door that held all of Mrs. Burke's messages fell off and the magnets scattered all over the floor. Then I started to swing back again.

"Aaaaaaaaaaaaah!"
I yelled.

I kicked and kicked,
trying to get a foothold
on the desk again. Instead
I knocked over the desk and
the chair. It made a big noise.
My fingers started to slip.

That was when Mrs. Burke led
the class up the hallway from recess. She
stopped and stared at me hanging there.

"What are you doing?" she asked. She wasn't
exactly shouting, but sometimes the way grown-ups
say something makes it seem like they are.

I let go and fell to the floor. All the pictures were
hanging on me, with my drawing of the dragon and
the gold egg right under my chin. The magnets were
spread out all over the hallway. The desk and chair
were lying on their sides.

The egg was still the wrong color.

As soon as I realized that I hadn't broken my legs

or anything, I started unwinding the string from my head and shoulders. Everyone was very quiet.

Then I heard someone giggle. I felt a laugh coming up in my throat, too. I was scared and laughing at the same time. It's a horrible thing when you're really in trouble and you can't help laughing.

Just then Mrs. Diaz and her first-grade class walked down the hall toward us.

Guess who was first in line?

Right. The Squid.

When she saw me sitting on the floor with the pictures wrapped around me, she put her hand over her mouth. I waved at her.

"Hey, Mabel, it's your brother!" a kid said. "He's so funny!"

All the other first graders shrieked like this was the funniest thing they'd ever seen. Then the kids in my class started laughing, too.

Almost everybody.

Mrs. Burke just shook her head and frowned.

I unwound myself from the pictures and stood

up. "I was trying to fix my picture," I said. "The egg was the wrong color."

"So you decided to pull everyone else's pictures down, too?" she asked.

I wanted to explain, but I couldn't think how to start.

She folded her arms and waited for me to confess. Everybody was watching and waiting to see what happened.

While everybody else in my class was just standing there waiting to see my life end, Hector the New Kid started gathering up all the pictures. He piled them all up neatly and handed them to Mrs. Burke.

She looked at him and smiled. "Thank you, Hector," she said.

When Hector gave her the pictures, it took Mrs. Burke's mind off of me for just a second and probably saved my life. She took the pictures from him, with the strings dangling down, and put them under one arm. Then Hector started to pick up the magnets. Pretty soon two or three other kids were helping him. I picked up a couple, too.

"Back in the room, everyone," she said. The class started to file in. I got in line and tried to sneak by.

Mrs. Burke put her hand on my shoulder.

I looked up at her.

"Is that your desk?"

I looked across the room. All of my things were spread out on my desk and on the floor around it from when I'd been looking for my pencils. I'd meant to put everything back, but I hadn't had a chance.

I nodded. Of course it was my desk.

"What happened?" she said.

"I was looking for my colored pencils," I said. "Samantha said the picture was wrong and it was bugging me and I couldn't stop thinking about it and I thought if I could just make the egg rainbow colored it would be all right but I couldn't get it down or reach it and—"

Mrs. Burke let out a long breath. "I'm not happy right now," she said. "What am I going to do with you?"

"I don't know," I said.

"Go clean up your desk and sit down, Charlie," she said, pointing to my seat. "I'd hate to have to call the superintendent."

Call the superintendent? The superintendent was like the king of all the schools! Call the superintendent? For pulling down pictures by accident? Was she crazy?

But I went to my desk and started to pick things up. Hector came over to help.

I looked at him. He smiled. I tried to smile back. After all, he had saved my life.

Then I noticed his hands. He had black marker all over his fingers.

I looked down at his new sneakers.

Yesterday they had been white, but now they were black.

"Why did you color your shoes?" I asked him.

He shrugged. "I wanted to."

11
Thanks to the Squid

"I can't believe you did that!" Tommy said when I told him about the great picture disaster in the hallway. He bonked me on the shoulder with his backpack.

"I didn't mean to!" I said. "It was Samantha Grunsky's fault."

"You should've stayed out at recess," Tommy said, climbing onto the bus. "Darren just kept talking about how you were a big chicken, and how slow you were."

"What a bozo," I said.

"Don't worry," Tommy said proudly. "I told him you were going to completely destroy him in the race. I told him you'd definitely race him tomorrow and you'd beat him by a mile."

"What did he say?"

"He said to just wait and see what was going to happen. I told him he was nuts."

I could already feel the wedgie Darren was going to give me. "Great," I said. "Thanks a lot."

"No problem." Tommy grinned.

If Mrs. Burke didn't kill me first, Darren would make my life miserable. Still, it would be nice to beat him. I was tired of Darren's bragging. I wanted *someone* to beat him, and I guessed it would have to be me. I wondered if I could.

"I just hope Mrs. Burke doesn't call my parents about the great picture disaster."

"Me, too," Tommy said. "If she does, it'll be the Great Charlie Bumpers Disaster."

Mrs. Burke didn't call my parents. But they still found out.

Thanks to the Squid.

As soon as we sat down for dinner, she blurted out the whole story of my hallway catastrophe. I didn't even have time to shut her up. I tried to explain to my parents, but the more I explained, the worse it sounded.

"I just wanted to fix the dragon's egg," I said.

Matt started to open his mouth. I knew he was going to say something to make me mad.

"Matt Bumpers," my mom warned. "Don't make this worse."

"I couldn't help it!" I said.

Dad just shook his head at me. "You're going to have to do better than that, Charlie," he said.

I was dying to ask him how he was doing with Mr. Grimaldi, but it seemed like a bad idea.

◆ ◆ ◆

The next day before recess I decided to ask to borrow a ball from General Shuler, Intergalactic Supreme Commander of Soccer Balls.

Mr. Shuler wasn't in the gym, but there was a new soccer ball lying right outside his office. I knew I shouldn't take it without letting him know. I found a piece of paper and a pen on his desk and left him a note:

The fourth graders have borrowed your soccer ball.
I will bring it back at the end of recess.
        Yours truly,
        Charlie Bumpers

Then I picked up the ball and ran out to the playground. Darren was already there with Tommy and some other kids, waiting for me.

"Ready for the race?" he asked, smiling his I'm-gonna-give-you-a-wedgie smile.

Boogers. I'd forgotten about the race.

"Wouldn't you rather play soccer?" I asked.

Darren wasn't very good at soccer, but I thought it was worth a try.

"Nope. Tommy said you were going to kill me in a race. So let's see you do it."

Just then, someone blew a whistle. We all turned and looked.

It was the Intergalactic Supreme Commander of Soccer Balls.

Mr. Shuler was marching straight toward me, and he didn't look happy. I wondered what he wanted—I'd left him a note about the soccer ball.

Everybody was watching us.

"Give me the ball, son," he said.

I handed it to him.

"Are you Charlie Bumpers?" he asked, looking at the note in his hand.

"Yes, sir," I said.

"Mr. Bumpers, weren't you the one I talked to the other day about borrowing gym equipment?"

I nodded.

"And did you not remember that I specifically told you to get permission first?"

"I remembered," I said.

"But when I went to ask your permission, I couldn't find you. So I left that note on your desk."

"That's not good enough," he said. "I want you to ask me in person."

"But—"

"No buts." He held up his big finger, which was attached to his big hand, attached to his big arm, attached to his big body. "If anyone borrows gym equipment again without permission, they're going to have to deal with me. And believe me, they won't like it."

Mr. Shuler squeezed the soccer ball with one hand. I imagined him squeezing my head until my brains came out of my ears. "Do we understand each other?" he asked.

"Yes, sir," I said, looking at the ground.

"Look at me, son," he said.

I looked up at him.

"Let's not have any more problems. Would you like to borrow the ball?"

"No thanks," I said. I didn't feel like playing soccer anymore. I didn't think anyone else did, either.

"Okay, then. I'll see you kids later in gym class." He turned and walked over to where Mrs. Burke was standing.

Before I knew it, Darren was at my side again. "How about racing now?"

I looked at him.

He was never going to give up.

"Okay," I finally agreed. I just hoped I could beat him.

Then I saw Hector the New Kid watching us and I got an idea.

12
Fastest Runner in Fourth Grade

"If we're going to have a race," I said, "we need some more runners."

"Like who?" Darren said.

"Caitlyn's fast. And so is Hector."

"Caitlyn's out sick today," Darren announced. "Who's Hector?"

I pointed at the new kid and everyone turned to look at him.

"We don't need him," said Darren. "This race is between you and me."

"Come on, Charlie," said Tommy. "I know you can beat him. I told everyone you were going to race!"

"Okay," I said. "One race. But Hector races, too."

"All right. Here's the starting line," Tommy announced, setting down two rocks. "You stand here and I'll run down to the finish line."

I took my place between the two starting-line rocks and so did Darren.

Hector was just watching, not saying anything. "Come on," I called, waving my arm for him to join us. He hesitated, then walked over slowly. I made room for him between Darren and me. Hector took off his glasses and put them in his pocket.

"I don't see why he's racing, too," grumbled Darren. "We're the fastest."

I ignored him. A few kids had stopped what they were doing to see what was going on.

"Now starting, the race of the century!" Tommy yelled in his sports announcer voice. He was standing at the far end of the blacktop. "The Championship Race for the Fastest Runner in the Fourth Grade!"

More kids had gathered to watch.

The three of us bent over, getting ready to take

off. We were so close to each other that our elbows were touching.

"On your mark…get set…go!" Tommy shouted.

We took off. I ran as hard as I could, pumping my arms up and down, trying to go even faster.

Some kids were cheering for Darren.

Some were cheering for me.

No one was cheering for Hector.

We were running neck and neck. When I looked, I could see that Darren was trying to slow Hector down by holding out his arm. I kept running as fast as I could, trying to keep up.

When we reached the finish line, I couldn't tell who'd won—it was really close. But I knew it wasn't me. It was either Hector or Darren.

"I won! I won!" Darren was screaming like he'd won a gold medal at the Olympics or something.

Hector the New Kid didn't say anything.

"No, you didn't!" Tommy yelled. "The new kid won."

"He bumped into me," Darren said.

"You were bumping into him," I said. "You were trying to block him the whole way! Wasn't he blocking you, Hector?"

Hector the New Kid just shrugged.

"It was a tie!" someone shouted. "Race again."

"Yeah!" everyone said. "Do-over! Race again!"

There was no way to figure out who had really won. It was too close. And since Darren was being so bossy, no one wanted to argue with him.

"Okay," said Tommy. "Everyone line up again. Go ahead, Charlie. You too." Darren and Hector jogged back to the starting line to get ready.

I wasn't really sure if I should race at all—the tie was between Hector and Darren.

"Hurry up, Charlie," Tommy said. "Get in line."

I headed back across the blacktop, but before I reached the other side I heard a whistle.

"Everybody inside!" Mrs. Burke called.

"But we're having a race!" Tommy yelled.

"Inside now! Recess is over," Mrs. Burke said, snapping her exploding fingers and pointing at

Tommy. "You can race back to the door."

"Forget it, Tommy," I said. "There's no point in arguing with Mrs. Burke."

"I see what you mean," he answered.

"Tomorrow," Darren said, "I'll beat you *and* the new kid."

I glanced over at Hector. He took his glasses out of his pocket and cleaned them off so he could put them on again. I wasn't sure, but it looked like he was smiling.

13
The Hazards of Toilet Paper

I thought and thought about the race that night and I was still thinking about it the next morning. By the time I got on the bus, I had decided.

"Tommy, I'm not going to race."

"Why not? The whole point of this is for you to beat Darren!"

"All we really want is for *someone* to beat Darren, right?"

"Well, yeah," Tommy said. "I guess."

"I'm pretty sure I can't beat him anymore. I hate to say it, but he's faster than me now. He's so much bigger! But I know *Hector* can beat Darren if he doesn't pull any of his tricks. I want to stand at the finish line so I can be the judge."

"Okay," Tommy said, frowning. "But Darren

will probably pull your underwear out of your pants again anyway."

"I know," I said. "But it'll be completely worth it if Hector beats him. The big problem is figuring out a way to make sure the race is fair. We have to be sure who wins. We need a better finishing line—something like that ribbon they break through at the Olympics."

"Right! But what can we use?" Tommy asked. "Maybe Mr. Shuler would have something—"

"No way. I'm not asking the Intergalactic Supreme Commander of Soccer Balls for *anything*. We'll have to come up with something ourselves." I thought for a moment. "It needs to be long enough to stretch all the way across the blacktop."

"I know! I know!" Tommy shouted. "What if we used toilet paper for a finishing line? That would work!"

"Genius!" I said. "But where are we going to get it?"

"We could ask Mr. Turchin if he would give us a roll."

I thought about that. I liked Mr. Turchin, our school custodian. Last year I'd helped him move tables and chairs around for assemblies a couple of times. Maybe he would help us. "Good idea. Let's go see him as soon as we get to school."

When the bus let us off, we went straight to the custodian's office. He was standing just outside his door.

"Hi, Mr. Turchin," I said.

"Good morning, Charlie. Good morning, Tommy. What can I do you for, my two fine gentlemen?" he asked, and started to laugh in his rumbly way.

"Is there an extra roll of toilet paper we could borrow?"

"Why? Is the boy's bathroom out?"

"No. We just need

it for a race we're having," Tommy explained.

"Toilet paper for a race?"

"Yeah," I said. "For the finish line."

Mr. Turchin looked at us and rubbed his chin, smiling a little. Then he scratched his head. "You're not going to make a big mess with it, are you?"

"No," I answered. "We promise."

"Because when someone makes a mess in school, guess who gets to clean it up?" He raised one eyebrow. "I'll give you a hint. It's not your mother."

"We won't make a mess," Tommy promised. "It's really important."

"All right," he said. "Let me see what I can find."

He went in his office and came back out with a full roll. "Listen to me, you two goofballs," he said, handing it over. "Do *not* make a mess with this!"

"We won't." I grabbed it and stuffed it into my backpack.

Mr. Turchin is a nice man. Anyone who gives two kids a roll of toilet paper without making a big deal about it is nice.

"Thanks a lot, Mr. Turchin," Tommy said.

"You're welcome, gentlemen. Don't do anything I wouldn't do."

I wondered if Mr. Turchin would use toilet paper in a race.

Maybe if he was in fourth grade.

At recess I took my backpack out on the playground. I didn't want anyone seeing the toilet paper until it was time.

Darren was on the blacktop, waiting for me. Other kids were gathering around. "Okay, time for the race do-over," Darren said. "Me and Charlie and the new kid."

"I'm not racing," I said. "You and Hector tied. You're the ones who should race."

"It's okay," Hector said to me. "You can still race."

"Nope," I said. "I'm not racing. I've got another job. Tommy and I figured out how to make sure we know who's officially fastest."

I reached into my backpack and pulled out the toilet paper. "The first one to break through the toilet paper at the finish line wins!"

Everybody started hooting and clapping. Tommy went to the starting line. I walked over to Hector.

"Don't stand too close to Darren at the start," I told him, "so he doesn't push you." I wanted to make sure that Darren didn't cheat.

Hector smiled and nodded. He took off his glasses, rubbed them with his shirt, and put them in his pocket.

I ran down the blacktop with the toilet paper with a few kids trailing after me. When I got to the place for the finish, I realized I needed someone to hold the other end.

"Can someone help me?" I called to the kids who were with me.

"I'll do it, Charlie!" Alex McLeod yelled out. "I can do it!" He was jumping around like someone had built a campfire in his pants.

"All right," I said. "But be careful."

"Okay, okay," he said.

"I mean it," I said. "You'll have to stand still."

"Okay, okay, I promise!"

"And we can't make a mess," I said. "It's Mr. Turchin's toilet paper."

Alex was hopping all over the place, grabbing for the toilet paper.

I let him hold onto the roll, then I very slowly pulled on the loose end. "Be really careful," I warned him again, "or it'll break." We unrolled the paper across the finish line and held it up as straight as we could.

By now it seemed like the whole fourth grade was watching.

"Okay!" I yelled to Tommy. "We're ready!"

Darren and Hector the New Kid lined up at the far end of the blacktop.

"Runners on your marks!" Tommy shouted in his Olympic announcer voice. "Ready...set...*go!*"

Darren and Hector the New Kid ran as hard as they could. Everybody was yelling. I yelled extra-loud for Hector, since I was worried that no one would cheer for him.

But some of the kids from our class were cheering for him, too. "Go, Hector!" they screamed.

Even a few boys from Tommy's class were cheering for Hector.

As the runners came closer and closer to the strip of toilet paper, I knew who was going to win.

Darren was big and fast.

Hector was small, but he was faster.

A *lot* faster.

It made me wonder if he'd been running as fast as he could the day before.

It wasn't even close. Hector won by a mile. When he broke through the toilet paper, everyone was going crazy.

They all surrounded Hector. Kids were patting him on the shoulder and back and yelling and hitting him on the head. Right then I knew he wasn't Hector the New Kid anymore. From now on, he was just Hector, the fastest kid in fourth grade.

It made me smile.

"Hector! Hector! Hector!" Everyone was chanting and jumping up and down.

Especially Crazy Legs Alex McLeod. He started running in circles, still holding the roll of toilet paper and shrieking. Somebody took hold of the loose end and pulled on it. It broke off and another kid grabbed the trailing toilet paper.

"No! No!" I shouted. I tried to catch up with Alex, who was now trotting around Hector. Everybody was still yelling and waving the toilet paper streamers.

"Stop it! Stop it!" I begged.

No one listened.

The toilet paper was spreading all over the playground.

I ran around trying to catch pieces of it, but it kept blowing away. Other kids held toilet paper banners up in the air like they were flying kites.

I never knew there was that much toilet paper on one roll. It seemed like it could stretch from here to China.

Or at least to Chile.

That's when I heard the whistle. Mrs. Burke blew it long and loud. And close.

Everyone stopped. Even Alex McLeod.

He was holding an empty toilet paper roll. You

never would have known he started it.

Ribbons of toilet paper were all over the black-top. Some of them were drifting around like fall leaves on a windy day.

"Where did all this toilet paper come from?" Mrs. Burke asked, snatching a wad of paper as it drifted past her. She really sounded angry. Angrier than when I pulled the pictures down.

Kids looked at each other. Most of them had no idea where it had come from.

It looked like Hector could get in the most trouble. Alex had wrapped him up in toilet paper like a cocoon and Hector was still pulling it off of his arms and legs.

"It's mine," I said.

Mrs. Burke turned to me. Her eyebrows scrunched down. "Where did you get it?"

I didn't really want to answer, but she

just kept standing there, squeezing the ball of toilet paper in her hands. I was sure she could wait longer than I could.

"Mr. Turchin gave it to me for our race," I said. "We weren't going to make a mess. We promised, but—"

"Hector won!" Tommy said before I could finish. "It was Charlie's idea, Mrs. Burke. He was the one who got Hector to race!"

The kids started yelling again.

Mrs. Burke blew her whistle again. "Please clean up the paper."

Everybody ran around and picked up the toilet

paper and handed all the scraps to Mrs. Burke. She held them for a moment, like she didn't know what to do with them.

Then she looked at me. "Everyone but Charlie can go inside," she said.

When the others headed back toward the school, Tommy didn't move. He stood there for a minute, waiting to see what would happen.

"Everybody," Mrs. Burke said, giving Tommy a serious look.

Tommy gulped and followed her orders.

Mrs. Burke dumped the bundle into my arms. Limp toilet paper streamed everywhere.

That's when the first graders came out for recess.

"Look! Look! It's my brother Charlie!" I heard the Squid scream. "Hey, Charlie! Where'd you get all that toilet paper?"

The other little kids went into hysterics. Say the words "toilet paper" and first graders all wet their pants laughing at the same time.

Mrs. Burke grabbed my arm. Her long fingers

had the grip of a monster wrench. She started inside, dragging me with her. Bits of toilet paper trailed along behind me. "Charlie?" she asked. "Was that a very good decision?"

Trick question! No good answer!

I shook my head. "We needed a finish line," I said.

"What am I going to do with you?" she asked. "Maybe I should just wrap you up with this toilet paper and bury you like a mummy!"

I knew it! She wanted to bury me like a pharaoh from ancient Egypt!

I didn't say anything until we were almost back to our classroom. "Hector was really fast," I told her. "We didn't even need a finish line to see who won."

She looked at me very closely and screwed her mouth to one side. She was probably trying to figure out where to bury me.

"I know all about you, Charlie Bumpers," she said, shaking her head.

We dumped all the toilet paper in the big garbage can by the door. I think if Mrs. Burke could have, she would have stuck me in there, too. Then Mr. Turchin could have taken me away with the rest of the trash.

We walked back into the classroom without another word. Everybody watched in silence as I went to my desk. Samantha Grunsky frowned at me like I was the lowliest worm on the planet.

When I sat down, Hector whispered, "Are you okay?"

I nodded. There was no use trying to explain to Hector how I felt. He was a nice kid and a fast runner, but he never made messes. He never got in trouble.

I didn't talk to anyone the rest of the day. I didn't raise my hand to answer questions. I didn't make any jokes. I did all my work. I was a good student.

I thought about being wrapped up like a mummy in toilet paper. At least mummies don't get into trouble.

Especially if they don't have Mrs. Burke, Teacher of the Year.

14
Dad Gets Serious
(or It's Not Funny!)

That afternoon, Mom picked us up at school. She met me at the front door, and the Squid showed up from her classroom a few seconds later.

"Charlie and Mabel, wait for me here," she said. "I have to check with Mrs. Finch about something." My mom helps out with the PTA sometimes, and she's friends with Mrs. Finch, the school secretary.

"Okay," I said. I was relieved, because I wanted to talk to the Squid alone for a minute. As soon as Mom went into the office, I got started. "Hey, Mabel," I said.

The Squid looked at me suspiciously. I never called her Mabel. "What do you want?"

"Um, you know that little thing with the toilet paper on the playground? I'd be really, really happy if you'd promise not to tell Mom or Dad or Matt about it."

She broke into a smile. "But it was so funny!"

"I know. But I'll get in trouble. I'll have to explain it, and they won't understand."

"I don't understand it, either," she said.

"That's what I mean. Just don't tell them, okay?"

"What if they ask?"

"Just don't say anything."

"But it would be lying if I knew something and didn't say it."

"Okay," I said. "If they ask, you can

say something. But if they don't ask, promise you won't say anything."

"Okay."

"Promise?"

"I promise."

"Okay," I said.

"Unless they ask."

"Mabel! They won't ask!"

"Then I promise."

Just then, Mom came out of the office. The Squid and I walked out of the school and got into our car. We were very quiet. Too quiet.

"What's going on?" Mom asked.

"Nothing," I said. I looked at my sister. Her mouth was shut tight. Too tight.

I knew if Mom asked one more question, my sister would blurt out the whole story. I gave the Squid a warning look. She clapped her hand over her mouth.

But Mom was already thinking about something else. She does that a lot, and right then I was glad.

The Squid's hand stayed over her mouth the whole way to our house. For once, she kept her lips buttoned. She disappeared into her room as soon as we got home. I guess she didn't trust her mouth to stay shut.

I was having a snack and Mom was starting dinner when Carla's mother dropped her off at our house.

As soon as the two girls came into the kitchen, Carla shouted, "Charlie, that toilet paper mess was so funny!"

I looked up from my snack. The Squid had her hand over her mouth again.

"It was sooo funny!" Carla said again. "Did you have to sit on the orange chair?"

The orange chair is where you sit when you've done something bad and you're waiting to see Mrs. Rotelli.

112

Mom glared at me. I looked up at the ceiling.

"Where'd you get all that toilet paper?" Carla asked.

I glanced over at the Squid.

"I didn't say!" she shouted. "I didn't say!"

"Didn't say what?" Mom asked.

"I didn't say about Charlie spreading toilet paper all over the playground. And I didn't say about everybody laughing. And I didn't say about Mrs. Burke being really mad."

"Mabel!" I yelled.

"She asked!" the Squid squealed. "She asked, and you told me if she asked I could tell, so I didn't break my promise."

Mom didn't ask me what had happened, but I knew I might as well get it over with.

I told her the main parts of the story, and when I finished she just shook her head and went back to her dinner preparations. She was slamming things around, so I knew she was mad.

I went up to my bedroom and tried to read a

book, but I kept reading the same sentence over and over again. A little while later, Matt came home.

"What's with Mom?" he asked, sticking his head into my room.

"She's mad at me." I put the book over my face.

"How come?"

"Because of the toilet paper," I said.

"What toilet paper?"

I told him.

He started to laugh.

"Ha ha ha. It's not funny!" I said.

"Oh yes it is," he said. "It's hilarious. I wish I could have seen it. Mrs. Burke must have killed you."

"Yeah, she did," I said. "Right now you're talking to the ghost of Charlie Bumpers. I might as well be dead."

That's when Dad came in the room. I could tell he was tired. He was probably tired of Mr. Grimaldi. Like I was tired of Mrs. Burke.

"Matt, why don't you head to your room?" Dad said.

"Can't I stay?" he said.

"No," Dad said, rubbing his eyes, which he always does when he's trying to think what to do. He looked over at me. "I don't know if I want to hear the whole story."

"I do," said Matt.

"Out, Matt," Dad said.

"But—"

Dad just pointed a finger toward the door. My brother walked out into the hall, but I figured he was probably standing right outside the door listening.

"It was just some dumb toilet paper, Dad." I tried to explain in a way that would make it seem better than it was.

Dad sat on the bed right beside me, his arms resting on his knees and his head propped in his hands. Then he turned his face to me.

"Charlie, I don't want to hear about anything else happening at school with you and Mrs. Burke. I don't care if it was an accident. I don't care if it was your fault or someone else's. You have got to straighten up. If I were Mrs. Burke, I'd be mad, too."

"I know, Dad, but I didn't mean for all that to happen."

"It doesn't matter, Charlie. You haven't been thinking."

I hate it when my dad gets really serious like that.

"You've got to use better judgment," he went on. "No one is getting you into trouble. You're doing it to yourself. You promised me you'd try to get along with Mrs. Burke, and using your head is part of getting along and staying out of trouble."

While he was talking, I looked down at the floor, then up at the ceiling. My dad would never have spread toilet paper around his office and gotten Mr. Grimaldi all upset. I didn't know what to say. I always have these great ideas I think will make things better, but things keep going wrong.

"I don't want to have to talk to you about this again. Do you understand me?"

I nodded but kept my head down. I felt rotten.

"Look at me," he said. "You've got to straighten

up. Pay attention to what you're doing, and don't do any more dumb things. Okay?"

"Okay," I said.

He didn't say it, but I was pretty sure he thought his youngest son was a bozo.

15

Teacher of the Year

When we came back to our classroom from lunch the next day, I saw my desk.

What I mean is, I noticed that it was messy again. Pencils and markers were scattered over the top. Some papers were hanging out and a few sheets had fallen on the floor.

I don't know how it happens. Maybe there are little guys who live inside my desk. They wait until I'm gone, and then they throw everything around and make a huge mess.

Anyway, I remembered what Dad said about trying. And I didn't want to fight with Mrs. Burke anymore. So I decided to stay in from recess for a couple of minutes to clean up my mess.

When everybody else lined up at the door, I

stayed put. *I must be insane,* I thought, *missing recess to clean up my desk.*

"Hey, Charlie," Hector said. "Aren't you going outside?"

"I'll be there in a minute," I said. "I have to do something first."

"I'll wait for you," he said.

"Go ahead and start the soccer game," I said. "I'll be right out."

Mrs. Burke came back in the classroom. I guessed she didn't have playground duty that day.

"What are you doing, Charlie?" she asked.

"Nothing," I said. Of course she could see I was doing something—I was cleaning out my desk. But I just didn't want to say it. It would sound like I was trying to be perfect like Samantha Grunsky or something.

Mrs. Burke nodded and didn't say anything. She sat at her desk and watched while I emptied mine and started to put things back. Then she started grading papers.

Just me and Mrs. Burke.

Missing recess.

I could see the playground out the window. Tommy and my other friends were playing soccer. Some first graders were throwing a ball up in the air and catching it right outside of our classroom window.

Hector was standing by himself. I wondered why he wasn't playing soccer.

I got everything back in my desk. It was neater.

"All done?" Mrs. Burke asked.

"Uh-huh."

"Charlie," she said, "we seemed to have gotten off on the wrong foot. But we're not very far into the year and we still have time to get off to a good start. I hope you'll pay closer attention to what you're doing and try harder to think about the consequences."

She stopped for a minute like she was thinking about something else to say. Then she looked outside. Hector was still standing by himself. She looked back at me. "Do you understand me?" she said.

I nodded.

"Now, hurry outside, or you'll miss all of recess. Use your head, all right?"

"Okay," I said.

"I know you can do better."

I nodded again and ran out the door of the classroom to the hallway. I was hoping I could still get in on the soccer game.

"No running!" she called.

I opened the big door and ran out onto the playground.

"Hey, Charlie!" someone called. "Help us!"

It was Brady, the crazy first grader.

"What is it, Brady?" I asked.

"Our ball," he said. He pointed up on the roof. One of General Shuler's new blue and white soccer balls was balanced on the edge, stuck in the gutter.

"Where'd you get that?" I said.

"I found it," Brady said. "Then I kicked it up on the roof by mistake. Can you get it down?"

"Where'd you find it?"

"In the gym," Brady said. "Can you get it down for us?"

I looked around. The Intergalactic Supreme Commander was talking with a second-grade teacher over by the gym.

If he saw Brady with the ball, the first grader was doomed.

"Can't you ask your teacher for help?" I asked.

"I did. She said she'll ask Mr. Turchin to get it down later."

The first-grade teachers obviously didn't know about Mr. Shuler, Intergalactic Supreme Commander of Soccer Balls. Neither did Brady. He didn't have any idea that his life was in danger.

"Can you please get it down, Charlie?"

Brady needed help. And fast.

I looked up at the

ball. I figured if I hit it with a rock, it might fall down.

I thought again.

Rocks are hard. And what if I missed and hit a classroom window?

I needed something softer to throw.

I glanced across the playground. Mr. Shuler hadn't seen us yet. Or the soccer ball.

The ball had to come down.

Somehow. Someway.

Time was running out. What if Mr. Shuler came this way?

I looked around for something else to throw. Then an idea hit me. My shoe was just the right size for throwing, and it wasn't heavy enough to break a window.

A bunch of the first graders gathered around me, watching me take off my shoe. Some of them giggled. They thought it was funny. They didn't know about Mr. Shuler.

I threw my sneaker at the ball. But my shoe hit the gutter and fell to the ground. I hopped over to where it was and picked it up.

Now the first graders were laughing and shrieking. I threw my shoe again. This time it hit the ball and knocked it out of the gutter. All the kids squealed and ran for it.

"Thanks, Charlie!" Brady yelled. He grabbed the ball and ran off with it.

I was a hero.

There was just one problem.

My shoe didn't come down.

When I backed away from the building, I could see it sticking up out of the gutter.

A kid screamed, "Charlie's shoe is on the roof!"

For some reason, everyone thought it was the most hilarious thing that had ever happened.

Funnier than a person covered in wads of toilet paper.

Funnier than a person hanging from the classroom door.

Maybe even funnier than hitting Mrs. Burke with my sneaker.

Ha ha ha.

Then I remembered exactly what she'd said to me last year in the hallway:

IF YOU EVER THROW A SHOE IN SCHOOL AGAIN, YOU'LL STAY IN FROM RECESS FOR THE REST OF YOUR LIFE!

Soon everyone on the playground was whooping and shrieking and pointing at my shoe on the roof. While I was standing there wearing only one shoe.

I felt like a bozo.

I *was* a bozo.

All the noise had attracted the attention of the teachers on the playground. And the attention of Mr. Shuler. He was marching toward us. Brady and another kid were kicking his new blue and white soccer ball back and forth.

"May I have the ball?" he said. They gave it to him.

"Where did you get this?" he asked.

They pointed at me. "Charlie got it for us!"

Me? Oh no!

Boogers.

General Shuler glared at me. "Haven't I talked to you before about gym equipment?" he asked.

"I was just…I mean, I didn't—"

The General didn't let me finish. "I don't want your excuses."

Then he looked down at my feet. "Where's your other shoe?"

I pointed to the roof.

I could see his neck was getting red. He had a big neck. A big neck connected to his big head and big shoulders.

Just then the fourth graders came up the walk, heading back to class.

Samantha Grunsky walked by. "Oh, wow," she said, "Mrs. Burke will just loooooove this."

When Tommy saw me with Mr. Shuler, his eyes got big. He tried to save me. "Charlie," he said, "I think Mrs. Burke wants you right now!"

"Not yet," Mr. Shuler said.

Tommy looked at me and shook his head.

"Go on inside," Mr. Shuler said to Tommy.

The last one in line was Hector. "Mr. Shuler," he began, "Charlie didn't—"

"Head on back to class, son," the General said.

"But—"

"No buts," the General said.

Hector gave me a sad look, then went inside.

Mr. Shuler looked at his watch and shook his head. "I have a class now," he told me, "but I'm going to talk with your teacher about your behavior. What do you think about that?"

Trick question! No good answer! I really wanted to explain but I didn't say anything.

"Get back to your classroom," he said. Then he turned and left.

But I didn't go back.

I didn't want to go back.

I wanted to disappear.

I sat on the step at the back entrance of the school and tried to remember a time when I had been in more trouble than I was about to be in.

I thought about the time I broke a glass door in my grandparents' living room when I was swinging a baseball bat in the house.

And the time I flushed Matt's cap down the toilet and water flooded all over the bathroom.

And the time I let the air out of one of the tires on my dad's car. By accident. With Tommy.

But this was worse. It was like everything I had ever done wrong had all been adding up.

Hitting Mrs. Burke in the head with the sneaker. The messy desk. The swinging on the door. The toilet paper. And now this—the shoe on the roof. After my dad had told me not to do any more dumb things. After Mrs. Burke had reminded me to use my head.

I was doomed.

The General was going to lock me in a smelly gym locker.

Mrs. Burke was going to keep me in from recess until forever.

My parents would never speak to me again.

I don't know how long I sat there—a pretty long time. I knew I should go back to class, but I couldn't do it. I was tossing pebbles into a crack in the sidewalk when I heard the door open behind me. I didn't look. I felt somebody sit down beside me.

It was Mrs. Burke.

Boogers.

She sat there for a minute without saying anything. Then she said, "You're missing a shoe."

"It's on the roof," I said.

"I heard," she said. "I asked Mr. Turchin to come out and get it."

"Thanks," I said.

"You seem to have a problem with your shoes," she said. Her face was very serious.

"I guess I do," I said.

Just then, Mr. Turchin came out the door carrying a ladder.

"Hello, Mr. Turchin," Mrs. Burke said. "One of my students seems to have misplaced his shoe."

"So I heard," Mr. Turchin said. He acted like it was a very normal thing for a shoe to be on the roof. I wondered if he'd had to rescue any other kids' shoes from on top of the school.

"Where is it?" he asked.

I got up and pointed out where it was.

He put the ladder against the roof and climbed up. "Here it is," he said. "Why'd you color it black? Were you going to a funeral?" He chuckled and tossed it down to me.

I put it on and tied it tight.

"You'd better put a double knot in it," Mr. Turchin said as he took down the ladder. "You don't want it to get away from you again." He laughed his rumbly laugh as he carried the ladder away.

Mrs. Burke and I didn't say anything. I felt all confused inside. Mad at myself, mad at Mr. Shuler, mad at the whole world. I could feel my eyes welling up with tears.

Finally I said, "I keep messing everything up."

A big tear snuck out of my eye, ran down my cheek, and hung on the end of my nose.

"I wouldn't worry about Mr. Shuler," Mrs. Burke said. "He's going to have to learn how to share the soccer balls. They don't belong to him, you know."

That was a funny thing for a teacher to say. I wiped the snot off my face with my shirtsleeve.

"Hector told me you were trying to help the younger children get their ball back."

I nodded.

"Throwing your shoe wasn't a very good choice," she said. "But it was very kind of you to help them."

I looked up at her in surprise.

"I know all about you, Charlie Bumpers," she said.

"What do you mean?" I asked. "You keep saying that."

She was quiet for a minute. Then she asked, "Do you know why I put you next to Hector in class?"

"So I would have a neat desk and be good all the time like he is?"

"No," she said.

"Then why?"

"Because I knew Hector would have a hard time when he started here. He comes from a long way away, and this is a big change for him. He needs people to be friendly to him. And when I asked the third-grade teachers who the friendliest boy was, Mr. Romano said it was you. The others agreed."

I think my face got red. Something inside me turned over. I sure hadn't expected her to say something nice like that. I smiled a little.

"Mr. Romano was right. You *are* friendly to everyone. And I needed someone to be friendly to Hector."

"That was easy," I said. "He's nice."

"Yes, he is," she said. "But if it hadn't been for you, Hector wouldn't have been included so quickly. He wouldn't have had the chance to do something he's good at and win the race. And other kids wouldn't even know his name."

I just nodded.

"It's a funny thing," Mrs. Burke said, "how sometimes doing something kind can get you into trouble."

I nodded again. That was a pretty interesting idea. And then I thought of something else. "Do I have to be friendly to Samantha Grunsky?"

Her face twisted a little, like she was trying not to smile. Then she said, "As friendly as you can be. Being mean doesn't really help anything."

"Okay," I said. I figured I could be a little nice to Samantha Grunsky if I had to.

"Now, Charlie," she said, "the things I said about

helping Hector and being friendly are our little secret."

"Okay," I said. I was feeling better and better. I doubted that Mrs. Burke shared very many secrets with her students.

"Any questions?" she asked.

"Yeah," I said.

"What?"

"Mrs. Burke, are you going to keep me in from recess for the rest of my life?"

She looked confused. "Why would I do that?"

"Because you said last year if I ever threw my shoe in school again, you would keep me in from recess for the rest of my life."

And then Mrs. Burke laughed. She laughed out loud. She put her arm around me again and hugged me.

"That was a joke," she said.

"It sure didn't seem like it," I said. "You sounded serious."

She shook her head. "Charlie, I have something

to tell you about myself. I have a very dry sense of humor and I can be very sarcastic."

I knew what that word meant. It means saying things you don't really mean in order to be funny. My dad can be sarcastic. He acts like he's serious, and it's funny if you know he's kidding. But you have to know him well enough to *know* that he's kidding.

I guess it was the same with Mrs. Burke.

Suddenly everything made a lot more sense. All her talk about her class being a prison and calling the superintendent and burying me like a mummy. It was all supposed to be funny!

"My dad's like that," I said. "And so's my brother Matt."

"Good. Well, then you understand. I try to be careful so people will know I'm kidding, but sometimes I'm not careful enough, and they don't realize I'm joking."

"Okay," I said. I knew right then I was going to get along a lot better with Mrs. Burke. I wondered how my dad was doing with Mr. Grimaldi.

"Are you ready to go back in?" she asked.

"Yep." But then I realized I still had one more question. "Mrs. Burke, how do you make your fingers explode like that?"

"Explode?"

"Yeah, when you snap them."

"You mean like this?" she said. Then she snapped her fingers. *POW!*

"Yeah," I said. "Where'd you learn to do that?"

Mrs. Burke smiled like she was remembering something. "I learned it from my mom. She was a teacher, too."

"It seems pretty handy," I said.

"Yes," she said. "It is."

We headed back to the classroom. As we walked down the hallway, she put her hand on my shoulder. *Maybe,* I thought, *it wasn't so weird that she was voted Teacher of the Year. I might have even voted for her if I'd had the chance.*

When we walked in the room, everybody was staring at us. I sat down at my desk. Hector looked at me.

"Hi, Hector," I said.

"Hi, Charlie," he said.

"Hey, Hector," I said. "Cool shoes."

He grinned. "So are yours."

Samantha Grunsky raised her hand.

"Yes, Samantha," Mrs. Burke said.

"What's going to happen to Charlie?"

Mrs. Burke looked at Samantha. Then she said, "Well, really, class, it's nobody's business what's going to happen to Charlie, but I might as well tell you the horrible truth. I suspect the police will be coming to my empire soon to put him in prison for throwing his sneaker on the roof."

She said it with a completely straight face. The class gasped. No one could believe it. Everybody started talking.

POW! POW! POW! Exploding fingers.

Everyone got quiet. Mrs. Burke looked at me. She raised her eyebrow, and the corner of her mouth turned up just a little.

I gave her a little nod, but I didn't give away our secret.

My best friend Tommy wasn't in my class.
Samantha Grunsky was. That was too bad.

But I had my new friend Hector.

And I had Mrs. Burke for a teacher.

And that was pretty good.

Look for the second book in the

Charlie Bumpers series!

Turn the page for a sneak peek...

1
A Big Part

"Are your desks cleared?" Mrs. Burke asked.

"Yes," everyone answered.

"Charlie," Mrs. Burke said. "What's that on the floor?"

I looked down. Somehow my math sheet had fallen on the floor. There was a sneaker mark on it. I picked it up and stuffed it in my desk. Mrs. Burke frowned and shook her head. "Okay, all of you thespians," she said. "Please listen carefully."

"What's a thespian?" I blurted out.

"Charlie, have you forgotten Rule Number Four of Mrs. Burke's Empire?" Mrs. Burke asked.

"Raise your hand," Samantha Grunsky said, sitting behind me.

I needed to know. I raised my hand.

So did Samantha Grunsky.

"I know what a thespian is," Samantha said.

That figures. Samantha Grunsky knows everything. Even stuff you don't need to know.

"Yes, Samantha?" said Mrs. Burke.

"It's an actor," Samantha said. I looked back at her and she gave me one of her I-know-everything looks.

"That's correct," Mrs. Burke said, "and today I want to talk about our play."

I squirmed in my seat. It was hard to sit still. Maybe she was going to tell us what our parts were in the play. I already knew the part I wanted.

Every year, each fourth grade class does a special project. Mrs. L's class designs an obstacle course for the whole school to run through. Ms. Lewis's class was making a special lunch with food from all around the world.

But Mrs. Burke's project is the best. Mrs. Burke's fourth-grade class presents a play. Everyone comes to see it. Even the parents. There are lights and costumes and props and everything.

My brother Matt gave me a hard time about the play when he found out I was going to be in Mrs. Burke's class. He said I'd probably have to be a bunny.

I did not want to be a bunny.

Last year the play was *The Elephant's Surprise,* and it was pretty good even though the elephant's cardboard trunk fell off halfway through the play and Mrs. Burke had to come out and hold it up every time the elephant talked.

But that was last year. This year the play was going to be *The Sorcerer's Castle.* Mrs. Burke read it to us in class last week. I really liked it.

There was a bunny in it, but it was a stuffed animal, so I was safe.

The Sorcerer was definitely the best part. I knew of four other boys who wanted it. And two girls.

Mrs. Burke picked up a big stack of papers. "I'm going to hand out scripts that will be yours to keep," she said. "At the top of the first page I've stapled a piece of paper that says what your part is."

This was the day! Now my legs were jiggling and my fingers wouldn't be still. Even my hair felt all tingly.

I *had* to be the sorcerer.

I knew that I could do the part really well. If I just got the chance.

Please give me the chance! I thought.

"Your first assignment," Mrs. Burke continued, "is to go through all the pages and underline the lines that are yours. Wherever you see the name of your character, underline that part."

Mrs. Burke started calling people up to the front of the class to get their scripts. I sat on the edge of my seat, ready to go. If she was going in alphabetical order, I would be soon, since my last name is Bumpers. But then I heard her say Cory Filkins, so she wasn't going alphabetical.

Boogers! I couldn't wait much longer.

The kids who had their scripts started whispering about their parts. I thought I heard Cory Filkins say something about "Sorcerer," but then Manny Soares said, "Me, too," so I figured they were the Sorcerer's assistants.

Finally, after a million years, Mrs. Burke called my name.

My heart was really beating fast as I walked up. She handed me my script. "This is a big part, Charlie," she said, smiling. "I know you can do it."

I nodded. This was a good sign. The sorcerer was a big part. Maybe I got it!

When I got back to my desk, I looked down at the piece of paper stapled to the top of my script.

I looked up at Mrs. Burke, then at the paper again.

It must be some mistake. I checked to make sure this was my script. "Charlie Bumpers" was printed on the upper right-hand side of the paper.

"The Nice Gnome?" I said out loud. "I *can't* be the Nice Gnome!"

BILL HARLEY is the author of the award-winning middle reader novels *The Amazing Flight of Darius Frobisher* and *Night of the Spadefoot Toads*. He is also a storyteller, musician, and writer who has been writing and performing for kids and families for more than twenty years. Harley is the recipient of Parents' Choice and ALA awards and two Grammy Awards. He lives in Massachusetts.

www.billharley.com

ADAM GUSTAVSON has illustrated many books for children, including *Lost and Found*; *The Blue House Dog*; *Mind Your Manners, Alice Roosevelt!*; and *Snow Day!* He lives in New Jersey.

www.adamgustavson.com